DREAMS WOVEN AS STORIES

DEVY PRAKASH MISHRA

Contents

CHAPTER ONE

Introduction

Brahmanand is a 34 year old young man, who is unemployed since last one year. Every day, he entertains himself by watching videos on YouTube. Sometimes, he also watches videos related to book reviews. One day while watching the book review video, he also felt like writing something, but, he had nothing to write, due to weak in writing, language, essay etc. and lack of interest in reading books, since childhood. Having little interest in worship, he knows little things, on the basis of which, he also makes people fool. Some days pass like this, but he is unable to write anything.

A few days later, at around 4 O'clock in the evening, watching the rain pouring out of the window of his pigeon-dining type room, whose monthly rent is five thousand rupees, he thought that why not in his dreams, he will go to that time, the works of which have been completely destroyed and about that works no one has any information. After this, he starts looking for mantras in the books, using which he can go back and forth in time in dreams. After efforts of many days and reading meaning of mantras, he got something. He feels that his work will be done by these mantras. He decides to use those mantras one by one. On searching the internet, he comes to know that places like Taxila, Nalanda, Vallabhi, Vikramshila, Mithila were the centers of education in ancient India. Where the knowledge of both Para and Apara Vidya was given. In his dream, he decides to go to the library of these universities. On the night of Amavasya, Brahmanand siddh the first mantra by chanting.

***

CHAPTER TWO

First Story: Apara

On the night of first day from no moon day, at 10 PM, Brahmanand lies on his bed and starts chanting mantra while meditating on the Vishwavidyalayas of ancient India. After a while he falls asleep and dreams that

'At dark midnight, he is walking with a woman towards her house. The woman is wearing a white sari of thick cloth. Her parents had passed away a few years ago. Now she lives alone in her house. Presently her financial condition is also mild. After walking little bit, that woman's house comes. The house of that woman is a huge building of many floors. There is only one big room on the ground floor. On one side of the room there are stairs leading to the first floor. They both go up the stairs to the first floor. There are many big wooden cabinets placed on the wall. The cabinets are fully adorned with a very large collection of books. All these books are in Bengali language. This collection belongs to the woman's mother.'

When Brahmanand's eyes open, it is 4 AM in the morning. Nothing happened in the dream as he had imagined, but he was not disappointed and starts writing his first story in day-

Somewhere in a village named Sangam, there lived a young man named Vishwas. His parents had passed away a few years ago. When his parents are alive. His father was a truck driver. His mother had a great desire to read books. Whenever his father came back to the village, he used to bring many books for his mother. In this way, he had many wooden boxes filled with books only. As Vishwas had no interest in reading, he never opened these boxes. Vishwas had unwavering faith in God. He used to observe Navratri fast and Ekadashi fast. He used to regularly visit the temple of mother Goddess situated some distance away from the village on Navami tithi. After offering prayers, he used to come back after performing Hawan in the Hawan Kund, which is built on single pillar platform, in middle of pound, in the front of temple, from where person performing hawan, is able see goddess deity inside sanctorum, when temple is open, and devotes are less inside the temple. One Navami he met a woman named Vidya, who was wearing white clothes, outside the temple but inside temple yard.

Vidya: I have been seeing you coming to this temple for many years. Which village are you from?

Vishwas: My name is Vishwas. I am a resident of nearby Sangam village.

Vidya: Looks like you have a lot of faith in Mother Goddess.

Vishwas: Yes.

Vidya: Looking at you, it seems that your financial condition is not good.

Vishwas: My parents passed away a few years back. I have a small farm in which I cultivate. Due to continuous loss in agriculture, my financial condition has deteriorated. When my mother used to look after farming, these fields gave very good yield.

Vidya: You did not learn about agriculture from your mother.

Vishwas: You haven't said anything about yourself.

Vidya: My name is Vidya. Why don't you request the Mother Goddess to improve your condition?

Vishwas: This is the result of some of my accumulated karma, due to which my luck is not supporting me.

Saying this Vishwas left for his village. Throughout the way he wondered why people were laughing at him.

The next day, in the afternoon, when Vishwas came back home after working in the field, he was surprised to see Vidya standing near his house.

Vishwas: You! how here?

Vidya: Wandering around, I reached here. Will you tell me the way to the temple from here?

Vishwas: Yes.

Vidya: I got tired of walking on foot.

Vishwas (laying out the cot standing outside the house): Come on, sit.

Vishwas went to the house to get water and something to eat, but there was nothing in the house except a small jaggery ball. Vishwas brought water and jaggery. Vidya drank water after eating jaggery. Vishwas was very happy to see Vidya eating jaggery and drinking water.

Vidya: Out of curiosity, a question has come in my mind. If you don't mind, I'll ask.

Vishwas: Yes, why not.

Vidya: How do you keep so many wooden boxes here?

Vishwas: These are the books which my father used to bring for my mother.

Vidya: If you do not mind, then I want to give a suggestion, which can bring some positive change in your financial condition.

Vishwas: Yes, why not.

Vidya : There is no library in this village and its adjoining villages. You start a library at your home and teach to those who do not know how to read and take three handfuls of rice for the fee.

Vishwas: Yes, the suggestion is fine, it will not cost anything.

After this Vidya got up without saying anything and went towards the temple. Vishwas did not feel hungry that day. This happened, two lunar months passed, but Vishwas did nothing. When Vishwas saw Vidya in the sanctorum of the temple, from a distance, while leaving the temple on a ninth from no moon day, then he noticed the suggestion given by Vidya. Coming back from the temple, Vishwas put all the books in the sun light, after that he put them separately, on the cot and box in the outermost room and walked into the room, keeping his mother's writings separate in the inner room. When he came out, he was very happy to see Vidya sitting on the cot, studying. Seeing Vishwas, Vidya gave him three handfuls of rice. Which he took directly into the brass bowl. After that Vidya started studying again. Vishwas had nothing to do with reading, he was only interested, in reciting a mantra, and reciting the seed mantras of Saptashati. He had only one brass bowl left with him, the rest he had already sold, so taking out the rice from the bowl for cooking, he kept the bowl very safe, and while chanting the Guru Mantra, he cooked rice and ate it and get satisfaction for the whole day.

The next day, when Vishwas came home from the farm in the afternoon, seeing Vidya studying, he too felt like studying. After washing his feet and hands, drinking water, he sat down to read with a book. Seeing him reading, Vidya suggested him to first read something written by his mother. Vishwas went inside to collect the articles written by his mother. When he came out, he could not see Vidya there. Vishwas started reading the articles written by his mother sitting outside the house. By reading these, Vishwas got complete information about his fields. When which crop should be planted in which field, how to take care of it, how which seeds should be prepared, how to grow which vegetable. Apart from this, he got the knowledge of, observing the changes in the weather, by observing the shapes formed by the clouds, and activities of the animals, birds and giving yoga power to his fields from, what he was interested in. Due to which his problem of farming was solved.

Vishwas started reading books every afternoon, seeing him, other people of the village also started coming to read books. Now Vishwas started running the library along with farming. Those who do not know how to read, he also started teaching them to read. Gradually his condition started improving. He also bought some animals with the profit he made from the library and farming. When he thought of buying some new brass utensils, he remembered the only old brass bowl left. When he took out the bowl, he was both sad and happy to see the bowl. The bowl was filled with rice and turned in golden bowl.

As time passed, the materially and spiritual balance was completely established in the life of the Vishwas. Due to which he could improve the life of himself and the villagers.

***

CHAPTER THREE

Second Story: Ichchha

On the night of second day from no moon day, at 10 PM, Brahmanand lies on his bed, and starts chanting mantra, while meditating on the University of Ancient India. After a while he falls asleep. When he wakes up it is 4 AM in the morning. Nothing happened as Brahmanand had imagined, but he starts writing without getting discouraged -

Once upon a time there was a village on the bank of a river, where before eighty years, from now there was no other means, except boat to go. At that time, a rich Brahmin family of high order lived there. Which was known for breaking the orthodox traditions from generations and for improving by balancing materially and spiritually. Pitamber was a young boy of this family. He loved village life. He never even thought of going to a far way big city. His bride's name was Santara and they both like orange very much.

Pitamber, loved Santara very much. She was tall, straight-faced, calm and unassuming. He had no envy, hatred and fear from anyone. She was very talented. She used to learn any work very quickly. She had learned daily chores like cooking etc. by watching her mother. Ever since Pitamber had brought Santara to this house after getting married, Santara had the responsibility of cooking and feeding the whole house. She never gave anyone a chance to complain. Even after a long time of marriage of Santara, she did not have any children.

The people of that village had never seen an aeroplane and the women had never even heard of it. There were many women in the village who had just heard about the train from others. They knew only bullock cart, ika and boat. Santara was also one of them. One day Pitamber heard about an aeroplane from outsider. After that, after completing the farming work, when he met Santara, he told Santara about the iron bird in which humans fly in the air while sitting. Hearing the words of Pitamber, desire of seeing aeroplane and sitting in aeroplane taken place in the Sntara's heart

After a long time, the Santara gave birth to a baby girl. She named her Shraddha. Santara used to take great care of Shraddha. The girl was 5 years old, but due to no school in the village, she did not go to study. One day when the Santara was doing some work in the courtyard, suddenly Shraddha came, and hugged the Santara from behind saying Amma-Amma. The Santara pampered and pulled Shraddha, towards the front.

Santara (gently moving her hand over Shraddha's head): My baby woke up. Did not wash face.

Shraddha (seeing, towards, working Santara): Nope. Amma, I dreamed today.

Santara (doing his work): My doll was eating laddoos, in a dream.

Shraddha: No Amma! I see very big house in dream. That house is liked as our one, but angna was very big. Something very big, like bird, white in colour landed in angna. The mirrors used in it were transparent. Inside, I was sitting in your lap. Amma! I want to sit in your lap.

Santara: Well, then who will does all this work, your grandmother.

Shraddha's Grandmother: NO! You mother and daughter take care. I will only enjoy.

Santara: What more my laddoo seen in a dream?

Shraddha (looking towards Santara): Amma! More (after a brief silence) all right. Its door opened. And taking me in your lap, you got down.

Santara (While doing her work, seeing towards Shraddha and laughing): The door opened in the air or on land.

Shraddha: No, No. In air. Then came down by the ladder. That also had some small wheels.

Santara (Doing her work): You counted the wheels or not?

Shraddha (with eyes closed): 1, 2, 3 .... three Amma.

Santara: Our daughter was travelling in aeroplane with her Amma in dream.

Shraddha: Aeroplane... Amma, what is the aeroplane?

Santara: The same, from which mother and daughter fly around and landed back in the yard, in your dream.

Shraddha: Take me for twirling on the plane.

Santara (washing Shraddha's face after finishing work): When I go, I will take you.

Shraddha (smiling): Amma, please buy red color white flower printed frock for me from fair, like I weared in dream.

Santara: Ok.

Shraddha: Amma, laddoos.

Shraddha's Grandmother: Laddoos are kept in Bhitre. Come and take the key.

When Shraddha turned 8, her mother died. After 2 years, Shraddha's grandfather fixed her marriage. But

Shraddha's grandmother did not like that family. Shraddha's grandfather fixed the marriage by saying that the boy is not like the rest of the family, he will take great care of your beloved. Unless your beloved has food to eat, he will not eat himself. Unless your beloved has clothes to wear, he will not take clothes for himself either.

After many years of marriage, when Shraddha did not have any children, the in-laws of Shraddha started pressurizing her husband for second marriage. When the pressure became too much, her husband got fed up and took her to the city. There they both started living in a rented house. Somehow, days started passing in poverty. After a few years, she gave birth, a baby girl. They both named her Paheli. Shraddha took care of her, like his mother used to take care of her.

Shraddha herself was not educated but she wanted to educate Paheli. For this she convinced her husband and got Paheli enrolled in a good school. After a few years, in the city where they lived, airport also started. Whenever an aeroplane passed over her house, she used to look at the plane with her head towards the sky. Time passed and Paheli passed the Masters exam and started looking for a job. But she did not get any kind of work in which she is interested. She got very disappointed. After about two years, she got job in the field related to her studies at a negligible salary. She was very happy with the work, but the low salary reduced her happiness. But she saw her future bright in that work, so she started working with full devotion. Due to less money for dowry, his father was not able to find the groom of her choice for her.

Almost two years passed like this. Paheli got an opportunity to interview for a job in a large private business association, which was far away from her city in another metropolis, where the language and food were completely different. Paheli took her and her father's sleeper class ticket in the train from the railway reservation center outside the railway station and on the pre-determined day, they both traveled by train and reached for the interview.

Paheli's interview went well. On the same day after the interview, both of them sat in the train to come back. On the seventh day from interview day, when Paheli checked her e-mail in the cyber cafe, she got the information about her hiring. She was very happy with this, but due to the low salary, she was also a little sad. When she went home and told this to her mother and father, both of them were very happy. Paheli telling, Shraddha about the train journey, expressed, her desire to go by plane this time. But Paheli's father refused. In the night when Shraddha and her husband were having dinner, Shraddha tried to persuade her husband.

Shraddha: The girl has a heart desires, let her go.

Shraddha's Husband: When did I refuse to go? Everyone should be self-dependent, irrespective of religion, caste, gender or class, it is the right of all.

Shraddha: You refused to go by plane. Please let her go by plane.

Shraddha's Husband (mildly angry): After a few years, I will get old. Both of us, are about to come out of age, have not even been able to buy own house, have not even been able to get Paheli married. I got nothing from home in your affair, at least a place to cover head I would got. Do whatever your heart desires.

Shraddha lowered her head and started eating food suppressing her laughter. The next day Paheli and his father went to the airport to get tickets. After going there, they came to know that the price of the tickets varies with time. The ticket price for each airline varies on the same day and time. All these can be viewed together on the websites on internet and according to budget and convenience they can book tickets from website.

On asking Paheli, the female employee sitting at the airlines window told her that the cost of a ticket for two people would be around twenty thousand. Hearing this, Paheli felt that it is appropriate to go by train only. Paheli booked train tickets for two people and started working on the predetermined day.

Paheli quickly acquired proficiency in the task. She used to learn any work very quickly and became proficient in it with self-study. Due to which she got a lot of progress in the field. Soon she got a job with high salary and after some time she also bought her own house. After everything was settled, she talked to her mother and father. She convinced them to stay with her. She also searched job for her father.

After this Paheli went home to pick them up. The next day after reaching home, after tying the luggage, Shraddha asked her husband and her daughter, if she should prepare something to eat in the train, then her husband started cleaning his shoe without saying anything with a smile, and Paheli also got busy in her phone, with her head down, with suppressing laughter. Shraddha asked again but both did not answer.

Shraddha: What happened? Why are you not telling? .... Paheli, tell me what should I make?

Paheli (looking at the phone): Me, I will not eat anything.

Shraddha's Husband: I too.

Shraddha: Fifty hours without eating and drinking.

Shraddha's Husband: Yes.

Shraddha: Any siddhi have been achieved, by you?

Paheli (laughs): I haven't got a train ticket.

Shraddha (in a light, loud and nervous tone): So, we have to go by bus? From here the direct buses goes.

Shraddha's Husband (in a serious voice): No.

Shraddha: Then?

Both did not answered and started pretending to be engrossed in their work. Shraddha standing in the room, once look at her husband, then Paheli, then again her husband then again Paheli, then sitting on the cot, she starts laughing at herself thinking something. Seeing her laughing, her husband and daughter both also started laughing.

Laughing Shraddha remembered her mother, and tears welled up in her eyes. The next day at 5 AM in the morning, they booked a rickshaw and went to the airport. Shraddha was wearing a red colour white flower printed sari brought by Paheli. Shraddha had never seen the airport from inside. Rickshaw dropped them near the arrival gate and left. Seeing Shraddha walking slowly and rapidly rolling her eyes around. Paheli grabbed her hand, and entered with her, from the entrance, and walked towards the check-in counter. After weighing their luggage there, they deposited the same. After this, after getting a security check, they went to the plane from the designated gate of the plane and sat in their places. Shraddha turned her head around for some time and saw the people and the plane, then listened to the instructions being given in the plane. In a while, the plane came into the sky. Like children, Shraddha started seeing the earth again and again through the mirror, it seemed to her that others would think that she had never sat in the plane before, so she kept quiet and sat down on her seat. She started chanting her guru-mantra mentally.

She slept while chanting the mantra. Till then Paheli too fell asleep with her head on her shoulder. They both dreamed-

'There is a house in the village, in the middle of which there is a big courtyard. In the courtyard, a small white coloured aeroplane arrives and lands. In it, a beautiful woman wearing a sari, with a child in her lap, is sitting on a chair near the mirror. The child is wearing a red colour white flower printed frock and looking out through the mirror. Outside the mirror, orange-yellow coloured laddoos of Bundi are kept in the jhaabiyaas.'

***

CHAPTER FOUR

Third Story - Bread and Thirst

At 10 PM on the night of third day from no moon. Brahmananda lies on his bed and starts chanting mantra, while meditating on the University of Ancient India. After a while he falls asleep. When he wakes up, it is 4 AM in the morning. Nothing happened as Brahmanand had thought, but he starts writing without getting discouraged –

Once upon a time, a young man named Roshan Mishra, lived in Lucknow, a city of Uttar Pradesh. He was well educated. He started working in a company, just a few days back, for Rupees 8000 a month. Everything was going well in his life. At the end of the first financial year his salary was Rupees 18,000 and on the completion of the second Rupees 28,000. Now his savings were getting better. Within a few months, he had collected some money to buy land. After seeing the land, he had decided everything by meeting the land owner. But the same day, at 3 AM in the night, he got scared after seeing the dream. When he went to office the next day, he was intimidated and asked to voluntarily resign. Due to being simple and straight forward, he resigned. He asked the land owner for an additional 30 days' time. Even after a month, when he did not get any success, he refused to take the land, telling everything to the land owner. Slowly 2 years passed, but he did not get any job and the money collected was almost exhausted. He became very disappointed and could not understand any right way to earn money. Then all of a sudden, he got an admission letter to appear in the written examination to work on contract in a company. Here he applied about three years back. It had been five years since he completed his studies. He didn't want to go for the exam as there was no preparation. But, when his mother saw that he did not go to Delhi, a day before the exam, she scolded him a lot. Due to which he got angry and left for Delhi at 8 PM without taking any money from home. On reaching the station, when he opened the wallet, he had only a Rupees 500 note with him. The exam was to start at twelve thirty am on the next day. He had never earlier traveled in a train, on an ordinary class ticket. He took an unreserved class ticket of Rupees 125 and went to catch the train on the platform. He stood for about 45 minutes but could not dare to board any train going to Delhi. When he tried in one, he got pushed behind. All the people in the ordinary bogie of the train were punched like straw. The condition of the sleeper was bad, even though, it was better than general class. Some trains on that route were canceled that day. It was 15 minutes past 10 in the night, Roshan was standing there. Just then, a man chewing betel, wearing glasses and hand made red colour half sweater, sat down taking the support of the pillar next to Roshan.

Person: A dumb, where will you go?

Roshan started looking around, there was no one except him and that person. He stood facing the other side. After sometime another train left from there and he remained standing there.

Person: Put the ticket in your bag and go back home. It is beyond your ability to go to Delhi today. Go home and try to meditate to achieve some supernatural power to travel without means of transportation, otherwise you will always be found standing here, and you will go back your home again.

Roshan got angry. But again he stood silently, facing the other side and waited for the next train.

Person: The next one is after 1 AM. Even if you catch it, it will be of no use. Yesterday, that train reached here, two hours late. Chandigarh Express will depart from platform number 6 of the narrow gauge at 10:15 PM. There will be no crowd till Moradabad. Descending Gajraula in the morning. Satyagraha will come there after 1 hour and 30 minutes. All the bogies in it will be of general category. It will reach Delhi in 2 hours. You still have 10 minutes.

Without thinking anything, Roshan ran towards the narrow gauge saying thank you.

Person (to himself without sound): Stupid, donkey, eight train left in front. Couldn't even board in any. For such people, even if the railway stopped the train by making a special announcement, they could not board. He is a stigma in the name of the boy.

Here, when Roshan reached the narrow gauge, it was completely dark on the platform and no one was visible on platform. There was no train on any platform. When Roshan saw the time, he felt that it was late. He missed that train. But a few minutes later he saw the train coming. Seeing the train coming, he went ahead. When the train stopped, he sat down in the adjacent compartment, on the chair next to the window. In the compartment, the chair in front of him was empty, in the rest of the place people were sleeping lying down. He too fell asleep with his feet spread silently. At 11 PM the train started. After a while, one boy got down from the upper seat to get lighter. While landing, his shoe fell on the man sleeping on the lower berth. Then that man wakes up and in anger ordered that boy to put down the shoe below berth, on that, the boy abused that man. Hearing the man's voice with anger, his wife sleeping on the seat next to him got up. On hearing the abuse words, the man given his one sandal directly on the boy face.

Man: I'll stop the train by pulling the chain now. I'll put you in jail. You touched my wife.

Boy (as if drunk): Yes, yes pull. Let me also see how much power there is in you and your Hidimba.

Seeing the manner of speaking of both, Roshan got a little scared. He felt that it should not be late in reaching Delhi because of them. Together with the rest traveler present in that compartment and next compartment, Roshan handled the matter wisely. The smell of alcohol was also coming from the boy's mouth while he was speaking. After all this, the boy went to the restroom. After coming from there, he drank water from Roshan's water bottle and talked with Roshan, then went to sleep. From the conversation, it came to know that the boy's wife is a teacher in the school and that boy works to bring advertisements for an advertising company. Roshan, got down at Gajraula at five passed half in the morning, and, after finding the platform of the next train, went to that platform. Where Roshan was standing, after a while Roshan found that, that boy was standing next to him.

Roshan: You, here?

Boy: There is some work in Delhi, I will go ahead after completing it.

The train arrived late, at 8 AM. They both got into the train. As soon as, that boy got into the train, he scold the person, sleeping on the upper berth, and, made a place for two people to sit on that berth, and they both fixed themselves on that place like rock and reached Delhi after 3 hours. After reaching Delhi, both of them used the accessible public toilet in turn.

Roshan: Now I go, otherwise it will be late.

Boy: It won't be late. Eat potato paratha with butter, drink tea, and then go by the metro.

Roshan was also hungry, he did not say anything. Both ate two parathas, drank tea. The boy gave money for both of them. Then the boy took tokens for both himself and Roshan from the ticket distribution window at the metro station. Roshan went to Okhla by Metro. Roshan was terrified of being late. He reached the center at one fifteen pm by auto for Rupees100. After seeing his admit card, the center operator logged in to the computer.

Operator: Just do what you can do in thirty minutes.

After thirty minutes Roshan logged out and came out. Then after catching the train, he came back home standing in an ordinary bogie, in which there was no space to breathe. A month later he was called for an interview and was hired. After two years his salary increased from Rupees 18,000 to Rupees 50,000 per month. He thought of buying the land again and after seeing the land, he decided everything with the land owner. That night he got scared after seeing a dream. His whole body was drenched with sweat.

First scene of the dream:

There is a fort in the desert. Roshan is sleeping on the bed in the topmost room in the highest tower. He is wearing silk, white colored, kurta, pajama. Black colored lines are made on the kurta. There is a pink colored bedsheet on the bed. The bed is bigger than the normal bed. On the wall just opposite the bed in the room, a white candle is lit on a tanish, made of two pegs and a wide strip of stone, and something is placed next to the candle. There is an open window in the wall next to the bed. Where standing, one can feel the movement of far and wide outside.

Final scene of the dream:

Roshan stands in front of Tanish, with his back, with his arms stretched out, sweaty, frightened, facing the window. His forehead is sweting profusely. He doesn't understand anything. He is shouting in a trembling voice "Begam, Begam.......". An old lady is trying to get in through the window, climbing up with the help of a rope, with an anchor stuck in the window. The age of the woman is around 80 years. She is wearing a pure white sari. There is no tiredness and weakness on her face, as if the old woman had reached there without any effort.

The next day, Roshan was intimidated in the office and asked for a resignation letter. He quietly resigned. He tried to get a job by staying in the same city for about 6 months. But he did not get any success. Due to the high cost of living there, he returned to his home. Every time Roshan's condition became like that of a thirsty person who gets only one sip of water. Each time at a very low salary, he would got job in the new field. As soon as the situation got better, the job was lost. Again he found himself at zero. Slowly, time was passing again. Somebody suggested Roshan to show the birth chart to astrologer. He took astrological suggestions from many astrologers. But there was no improvement in the situation. In a few words, one of his friends told that if Rahu and Mars are bad, there is also a danger of using Tantra. He was a man who believed in Karma. He didn't pay heed to that friend. After a few more days, Roshan once thought of doing a broom, and traced the exorcist. He went to the exorcist's place. The exorcist was sitting on the bed of the reed. About 25, 26 people were sitting on the ground on all three sides, talking about their problems. The exorcist was giving clove, camphor to people to throw and burn. People were going back putting money in his pocket. Roshan stood by giving an empty space near the cot.

Exorcist (looking at Roshan): Sit down. Will take time.

Old Amma (looking at the Roshan): Betvva, it is your turn after us.

Exorcist: I sit at four in the morning and sit till 12 in the night.

A girl: Baba, it is so crowded in the morning also?

Exorcist (looking at Roshan): No. At 6 AM, it is easy to talk.

A woman: My boy has a very high fever and does not listen my words.

Old Amma: Yes, the boy is very ill.

Exorcist (laughs): Hey, I will fix everything.

A girl: Baba, do my work, I am getting late, I am coming from college without informing at home.

Exorcist (taking out all the money from pocket and giving it to the girl): Count it.

A girl (after counting) : Three thousand only.

Exorcist: If someone wants change, then take from her.

After giving change, the girl gave six, five hundred notes to Exorcist.

A girl (showing photo of boy): I am not getting married. No one is accepting.

Exorcist: Eat this clove every morning on an empty stomach. The marriage will be fixed in 60 days and your mind will also start functioning properly.

Similarly, 2 hours passed. Roshan did in and out many times in such a long time.

Exorcist (looking at Roshan): Will continue to do Kathak all the time? Sit at one place quietly.

Then 4 boys from the village came.

Elder boy (touching feet): Baba, don't know where the buffalo has disappeared?

Exorcist: Went to work in a closed factory. Can't come, go bring buffalo.

Elder boy (putting 2 coin in Exorcist's pocket): Baba, if I come at leisure, then I will sit.

After a while it started getting dark. Roshan came back. After 7 days, in the morning, he went again. Baba was sitting on the ground outside the house. A boy was sitting in front of him and the boy's father was standing.

Exorcist: Bira has exploded. Where are lemons?

Boy (giving lemons): Yes.

Exorcist (Blowing, four lemons): After moving seven times around your head, throwing each one in all four directions.

The boy's father took all the four lemons.

Exorcist (seeing the boy picking up the remaining lemons): Leave some for me too. Beera will not be cut by your throwing. I have to do something.

Both left from there. Roshan was standing away and looking around silently, everyone. Now Roshan went and sat in front of Exorcist.

Exorcist (looking at the bamboo): This, which has become like a thin branch in the bamboo, thorn it.

Roshan (picking up the sickle kept near the exorcist and standing near the bamboo): Which one?

Exorcist (pointing with finger): That one, ..., this too.........

After this, the exorcist, ordered Roshan to clean the place where the exorcist was sitting. After cleaning of that place, without listening Roshan's problem, the exorcist blew camphor and gave it to him to burn. When Roshan was coming back, he found a milkman on the way.

Milkman: Why you trying these things?

Roshan: How you know?

Milkman: I know everything. If you fall into all this, your life will be ruined. Nothing will be achieve by you, everything is only karma, by dedicating everything to the goddess, do your work. For your satisfaction, I will show you the house of a Pandit ji. If you want, then met him.

After a few more days, Roshan went to Pandit ji's place. As soon as he reached he touched his feet and told the problem.

Panditji: There is a fault.

Roshan: What? What to do?

Panditji: Everything is Karma. It's open, enjoy. If there is a lot of problem, then (pointing with the hand) I can made it this much small by chanting and doing Havan.

Roshan: How much will it cost?

Panditji: Rupees 1,500. Will take 3 days.

Roshan: Surely, I will get a job after that.

Pandit ji: Yes. But you will join or not it depends on you.

Roshan: I will.

On giving money, Pandit ji read out the resolution. On the third day everything was completed in a day. Roshan dreamed again in the night.

Dream Introduction:

Roshan lives in a very beautiful country. There were people following only one religion from the beginning. On the basis of the teachings and researches of that religion, that country had progressed a lot. But gradually the new generation people found it very difficult to live life on the basis of those teachings and they abandoned it. Whatever possible for some people, they kept trying to follow those rules. Due to which the highest Vidya in that country disappeared forever. After its disappearance, the number of people who did not believe in this religion became very large and they came to power. Coming to power, they dissuaded the Brahmin class of that religion from the work of education and rituals and confined them to the work of wages. New language, education system practiced. All old literature destroyed. A large number of machines were manufactured for the work of wages. Due to which the Brahmins of previous system got less work of wages and they were left with no other way but to beg for a living.

First scene of the dream:

It is evening. Roshan, along with one of his female friends, is walking around the market talking slowly, here and there. There an old woman dressed in a dirty white sari is begging. The old woman holds Roshan's feet and asks for bread to eat. Seeing her, Roshan felt that the old woman was hungry for a long time. But Roshan scolds the old lady and goes to her house laughing. Her house is on top of a multi-storeyed building. After reaching Roshan's house, the old woman dies due to hunger. That old woman had begged last time for bread from Roshan .

Second scene of the dream:

It's night time. Roshan is sleeping in his room. The window of his room is open. There is a vault in the front wall. An old woman wearing a black sari is trying to enter his room through the window, with the help of a rope. That old lady is bald. That old lady has a long chutiya in her head. Roshan wakes up suddenly and gets very scared seeing that old lady.

Third scene of the dream:

Roshan is looking at the old woman in front of the open vault, with both hands outstretched, facing the window. A candle is burning in the safe. A dry bread is placed next to the candle. He is shouting in a trembling voice "Begam, Begam, Begam..........."

Even seeing the dream, Roshan woke up. In the morning, he made a roti or bread and fed it to the cow He donated pulses, rice, wheat powder, jaggery, salt, fruit, money in the temple and asked for forgiveness from inert, conscious, non-moving, moving creature for whatever troubles he had caused to them in any time and space. About 15 days later, he was called for an interview for the government job exam written 4 years ago, but then a pandemic broke out and a nationwide shutdown was announced. Due to which the interview got postponed. 90 days later, slow down started in shutdown. Then he got work in a new area for 180 days. After this, Roshan himself started taking contracts for small works. Gradually his condition improved and he never had to look back in life.

***

CHAPTER FIVE

Fourth Story - Boon and Curse

At 10 PM on the night of fourth day from the no moon day, Brahmananda lies on his bed and starts chanting mantra while meditating on the University of Ancient India. After a while he falls asleep. He has a dream in his sleep. When he wakes up it is 4 AM in the morning. Nothing happened as Brahmanand had imagined, but he sits down to write when he gets time without getting disappointed, but is unable to make any story on the dream. After a long time, he decides to just write the dream.

Introduction of Dream:

Out of the countless objects rotating in the universe, there was once life on an unknown celestial body. The inhabitants of that celestial body believe in only one religion from the beginning and follow all the arrangements or rules, however unfavorable they may be. For them, every work is a means to worship the formless supreme. The society, there is divided into four varnas and varnas into castes, castes into sub-castes, on the basis of varnas, there is written exam and karma is determined by the performance in that exam for whole life. On the same celestial body a new young man named Taamr also lives. He doesn't like this arrangement at all. He belongs to the fourth varna and most of the population of that varna comes in the lowest class sub-caste, whose life is very miserable. They don't have any rights. It is mandatory for them to marry and have children till the age of 21. Even after working hard and in filth all day long, it is difficult for them to get enough clean and good food grains every day for one time. They mostly have to run from the food left by others here. The houses of their community have been built outside the city. All the people of 18 to 21 years of this class get the opportunity to take the exam only once for the determination of karma. Only 10 percent of the people are passed in this. By keeping the unqualified people in the lowest category, their life is made like hell forever. This time Taamr has also turned 18 years old. He hates the Brahmins, there very much. He feels that this wrong system has been made by Brahmins to fulfill their selfishness. They always want to maintain such a class in the society which is economically suppressed, uneducated, artless and being more members in the family is ready to do any kind of work under any circumstances. So that, showing the greed of money and fear of religion, exploiting the society according to them, they continued to live their life happily.

First scene of the dream:

Taamr is giving written examination in a very large examination hall. After some time all the examinees submitted both the question paper and the answer sheet and start leaving the room. In the end, Taamr also comes out. The building containing examination hall is built on a very large plot of land. At some distance from that building, three small rooms have been built on the same plot of land. Where the concerned officers sit.

Second scene of the dream:

Taamr is roaming here and there. There are four or five more youths roaming around. Taamr goes and stands near a Peepal tree. There are also some shrubs nearby. There is, also a weak, rudimentary Ber tree among these shrubs. A servant is going on foot to the concerned officer's room, taking the set of first pages of the answer sheets, on which the roll number, the marks obtained in each question, the sum of the marks are written. These pages are sorted according to total marks obtained. As soon as servent reach the Peepal tree, Taamr's friends confuse the servant for a few moments. In those moments, Taamr takes out one-fourth of the pages from the servant's bag and throws them in the bushes near the Ber tree.

Third scene of the dream:

Taamr's friends have left. Sitting under the peepal tree, Taamr wandering his eyes around the campus, thinking about something. All the students have left the campus. After some time he realizes that he has committed a great sin. For his own benefit, he has made arrangements to make the life of many deserving people and their families, like hell. He feels very sad. He starts thinking of a way to correct his mistake.

Fourth scene of the dream:

Taamr starts walking towards the concerned officer's room. He is thinking about what he will say after reaching there. On reaching the door of the room, the officer scolds him and drives him away without listening. Taamr feels very bad. He gets back from there silently.

Fifth scene of the dream:

A sad Taamr, is walking in a deserted field hurriedly, thinking about something. It's almost dark. Then he falls due to a stumbling block. When he wakes up he finds himself in the forest. There is sunlight all around. Where he is standing, there is a source of cold and sweet water nearby. In the surrounding trees, there are some fruit trees. There is a very dense and big Peepal tree just in front of it. Around which there is a place to sit and sleep by placing a pile of soil. Taamr looks around there. He find himself alone in the forest. He likes the forest very much. Sitting in a half lotus pose, he laughed like a sannyasi pretending to meditate, slept in the corpse posture, ate fruits and flowers and drank sweet water. One day he hears a mantra in his sleep. He starts trying to chant that day and night. While chanting the mantra, he gets to know the method of Kundalini sadhna. Now he starts doing both penance and chanting. After many days have passed, suddenly desire to eat dish come in him. As soon as he meditates on the dish and chants the mantra, the dish appears in front of him in a golden utensil. He is very happy. Now he can create and dissolve anything just by will in him.

There is no hatred, anger, ego left in him. Sometimes trees, plants, birds also talk to him. One day while doing penance, he felt that someone was standing in front of him. When he opens his eyes, a slender old Brahmin, wearing a yellow janeo on his shoulder, and red dhoti, standing in front of him with the help of a stick. He gets angry seeing the Brahmin.

Brahmin: Bhikshaam dehi.

Taamr: Are everyone dead in the city, have you come to rob the forest? Looking at you, it seems that there is no one left in the city to exploit. You are only in such a position or all other robbers.

Brahmin: Bhikshaam dehi.

Taamr: How are you, who chant mantras and meditate but not capable to satisfy own hunger..... All your life you have just pretended. (In high voice) You guys should be put in the dungeon. (In a very high voice) Look, I will show you, what is mantra? what is chanting? what is austerity? what you want?. Look, you will see.

As soon as this is spoken, many different grains, fruits, dishes, sweets appear in front of the Brahmin in golden utensil.

Taamr: The hypocrite, the one who lives on the labor of others, (in a very high voice) dhuart, pick up what one wants.

Brahmin (opening the mouth of the bag): Bhikshaam dehi.

Taamr (taking out a long breath): I have to put it in your bag. You won't even take it, yourself. All this will come in your bag too.

One by one the Taamr put everything in the bag of the Brahmin. Everything got absorbed in it.

Brahmin: Kalyanam Astu, son.

Taamr: You will die while taking all this to the city.

The brahmin quietly walks away from there. As the Taamr lowers his head, the Brahmin disappears.

Last scene of the dream:

Taamr again closes his eyes and sits in a half lotus pose. After a while his face becomes calm. And suddenly bright light is visible to him through closed eyes. That bright light says – "You will be a Brahmin by birth in your all lifes. You will get everything before you feel the need."

When Taamr opens his eyes, he finds himself in the same field, in the same condition where he stumbled and fell. Then some soldiers passing from there, recognize him and put him in jail.

***

CHAPTER SIX

Fifth Story – Chakamak

At 10 PM in the night on fifth day from the no moon, Brahmananda lies on his bed and starts chanting mantra while meditating on the University of Ancient India. After, a while, he falls asleep. When he wakes up, it is 4 AM, in the morning. Nothing happened as Brahmanand had imagined, but he starts writing without getting discouraged –

Out of the innumerable bodies rotating in the universe, somewhere, on an unknown celestial body, where only, the sand of the desert is visible far and wide, there lives a new young man named Chukam, who is very simple, true and beautiful. Two types of people live in this desert by forming separate states. One who considers only their religious beliefs to be correct. Those who do not follow their principles, these people destroy them by consider it their duty. These people call themselves 'White Puja' and other types of people they call 'Lal Lakshya'. These people always try to destroy the 'Lal Lakshya' by attacking them, but so far they have not succeeded.

Chukam is a boy who lives in his own world away from all this. He looks very handsome in white kurta. One day while shopping with his mother in the market, he sees a girl named Neelam, who is shopping with her mother at that place. The mother of both of them know each other, but they do not like each other. Neelam and Chukam fall in love with each other at first sight. Chukum and Neelam start visiting each other's house on some pretext and start meeting each other secretly. Chukum's mother does not like Neelam. With the passage of time, Neelam-Chukum's friendship and love intensify. But Neelam's father arranges her marriage to someone else without informing Neelam. When Chukum and Neelam come to know about this, they both run away and get married. After marriage, their family members throw them out of the house. They both steal from their respective homes and go to distant cities, where no one knows them. They both start living in a rented room. The stolen money is almost gone in a few days. But they have not got any work from which they can earn their living. Chukam have knowledge of several languages. Then he starts entertaining people by dressing up in different guise, speaking different languages, playing gimmicks on the street with Neelam. One day, a minister from there, noticed the Chukam doing a gimmick. The minister is greatly impressed by Chukum's talent. After getting to know everything about Chukum from his employees, he calls Chukum to meet him. The minister, introducing himself to Chukam, greatly praises him for his knowledge of language and disguise skills.

Minister: Will you work for me?

Chukum: As you order. Please explain about work, I will start from now.

Minister: Not now. There is a lot of danger at work. You will have to stay away from Neelam for a long time. If the work is done right, then you will get a lot of money, name and palace from the emperor.

Chukam (in a sad tone): I will has to stay away from Neelam for a long time.

Minister: Never mind. We are in no hurry. You discuss with your wife before taking decision. But remember, your life will be completely changed. All the troubles will end for forever. Money, so much that both of you cannot even think together.

Chukam went home and discussed with Neelam, then said yes to the minister. The minister gives Chukam and Neelam a house to live in. Starts Chukam's training and gets Neelam to do some minor work. At the end of the training, the minister gets Chukam to enter the enemy's kingdom disguised as a Brahmin. Chukam, wandering there for some time, impressing the people with his knowledge and skills, learns new techniques from the knowledgeable people there, comes in contact with the people close to the king there. Gradually, by pleasing the entire royal court with his knowledge and conduct, he also gains the trust of the king. Now he starts getting a lot of secret information too. Who goes there to reach his minister. On the basis of that information, the minister makes full preparations for the attack and attacks the 'Lal Lakshya'.

As the war is almost over, Chukam gets a message to return. The minister sends Neelam to welcome, Chukam. Neelam welcomes Chukam and walks with him towards her palace. There is a congested area on the way. Chukum feels that the people, there, are staring at him.

Neelam: Why are you so scared?

Chukam: May be they kill me, assuming, someone else.

Neelam (with smile on face): Your hat is hiding, your chutiya. Do not afraid. The minister has called to meet. The minister has given us a palace. Now we are going straight to the palace.

After reaching the palace, Chukam first takes rest. Then at night goes to meet the minister.

Minister: You have done a commendable job. The king is very happy with you.

The minister takes Chukam to the desert where the war has taken place. The sand there has become red after drinking the blood of enemies. Dead bodies are lying grovel in the sand all around. Seeing them, it seems as if ordinary people are disguised as soldiers. Everyone has a red colored turban on his head, which has dried up after getting drenched in the blood, coming out of the hole made on the head passing weapon from top of the turban. Chukum gets very upset seeing all this. One of those dead bodies raised his face slightly and looking at Chukum said - "You have deceived us." It didn't take long for Chukum to recognize him. When he had entered the enemy's kingdom in disguise, he first had friendship with him, from him, he had learned to do many harsh secret practices. He regrets that in the greed of money and material comforts, he used his skills to do mischief. Filled with remorse, drowning in grief, he falls on his knees in the sand. His head hangs down completely, and, he starts crying bitterly. Seeing this condition of his, minister, who standing behind him does not take long to understand that now Chukum become a headache for him. The minister, without wasting a moment, takes out his sword from the sheath in anger and, with full force, beheads the grieving, unarmed Chukum from behind at once. Chukam's head separates from his torso and falls right next to the head of his wounded friend, who is grovel in sand. On seeing Chukam's severed head, his friend, who is injured and grovel in sand also dies.

***

Printed by Libri Plureos GmbH in Hamburg,
Germany

9 798887 728483